# When God Made You

Matthew Paul Turner    illustrated by David Catrow

WATERBROOK

*For Elias, Adeline, and Ezra*

—MPT

*To Beetle*

—DC

WHEN GOD MADE YOU

Hardcover ISBN 978-1-60142-918-6
eBook ISBN 978-1-60142-919-3

Text copyright © 2017 by Matthew Paul Turner
Illustrations copyright © 2017 by David J. Catrow

Cover design by Mark D. Ford

Published in the United States by WaterBrook, an imprint of the Crown Publishing Group, a division of Penguin Random House LLC, New York.

WATERBROOK® and its deer colophon are registered trademarks of Penguin Random House LLC.

The Cataloging-in-Publication Data is on file with the Library of Congress.

Printed in the United States of America
2017—First Edition

10 9 8 7 6 5 4 3 2 1

SPECIAL SALES
Most WaterBrook books are available at special quantity discounts when purchased in bulk by corporations, organizations, and special-interest groups. Custom imprinting or excerpting can also be done to fit special needs. For information, please e-mail specialmarketscms@penguinrandomhouse.com or call 1-800-603-7051.

You, you, when God made YOU,
God made you all shiny and new.

An incredible you, a you all your own,
a you unlike anyone else ever known.

An exclusive design, one God refined,
you're a perfectly crafted one of a kind.

'Cause when God made you,
somehow God knew
that the world needed someone
exactly like you.

You, you, God thinks about you.
God was thinking of you long before your debut.

From the very beginning, amid history and time,
you, little one, never left God's mind.

God imagined your eyes,
your head's shape and size,
and knew what you'd look
like when you felt
surprised.

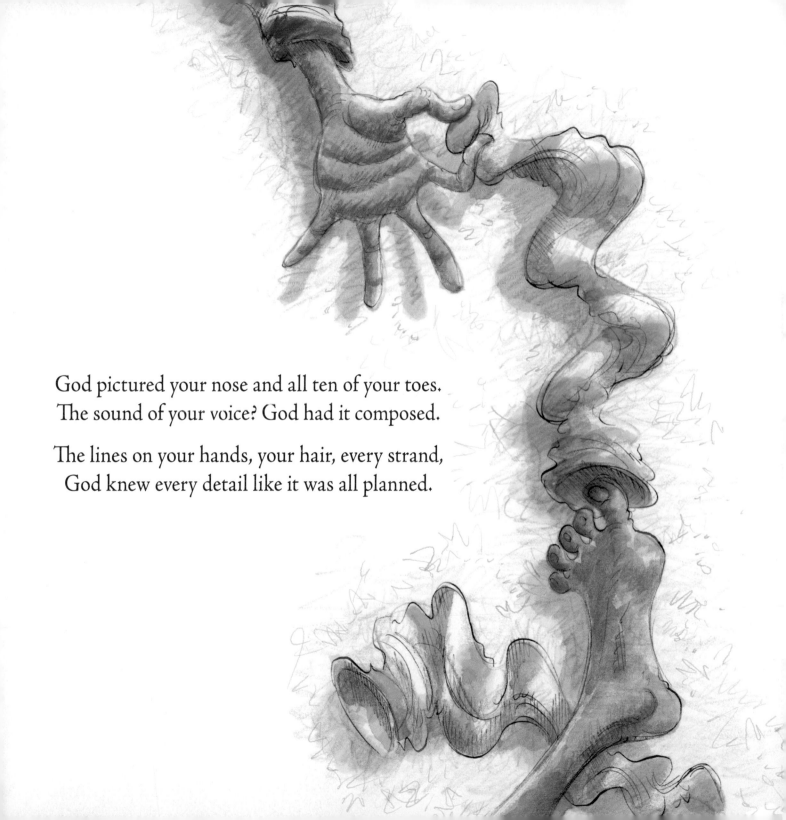

God pictured your nose and all ten of your toes.
The sound of your voice? God had it composed.

The lines on your hands, your hair, every strand,
God knew every detail like it was all planned.

Out of billions of faces from cultures, all races,
people God made, from all different places,

God knew your name. Your picture is framed.
God's family without you would not be the same.

'Cause when God made you, this much is true,
the world got to meet who God already knew.

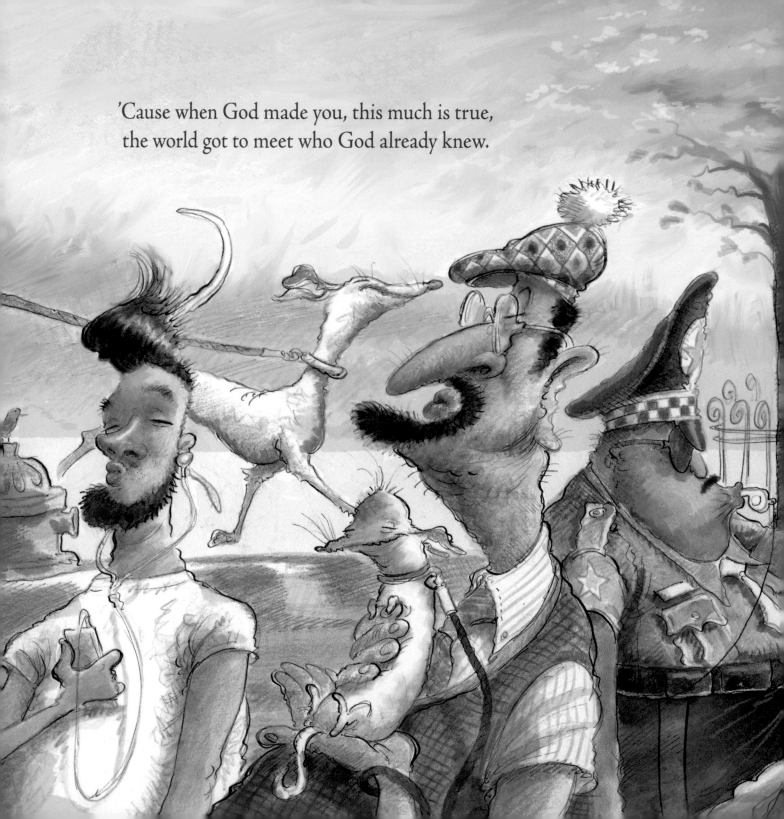

You, you, when God sees you,
God delights in what is and sees only what's true.

That you—yes, YOU—in all of your glory,
bring color and rhythm and rhyme to God's story.

So be you—fully you—
a show-stopping revue.
Live your life in full color,
every tint, every hue.

Discover. Explore!
Have faith but love more.
And learn and relearn all
that God made you for.

Use your talents and passions,
those gifts that God fashioned.
Think up ideas and then
put them to action.

'Cause God loves you creating, your true self displaying,
when light on the inside through art is portraying.

When you make-believe, the stories conceived,
the heroics, the magic, those tricks up your sleeve.

When you dance alone,
spinning like a cyclone,
being whoever, whatever,
in a world all your own,

God smiles and here's why—in the spark of your eye,
a familiar reflection shines bright from inside.

'Cause when God made you
and the world oohed and aahed,
in heaven they called you an image of God.

You, you, when God dreams about you,
God dreams about all that in you will be true.

That you—God's YOU—will be hopeful and kind,
a giver who lives with all heart, soul, and mind.

A dreamer who dreams in big and small themes,
one who keeps dreaming in journeys upstream.

A mover, a shaker, a lover of nature.

A builder of bridges, you, the peacemaker.

A you who views others as sisters and brothers
and lives by three words: love one another.

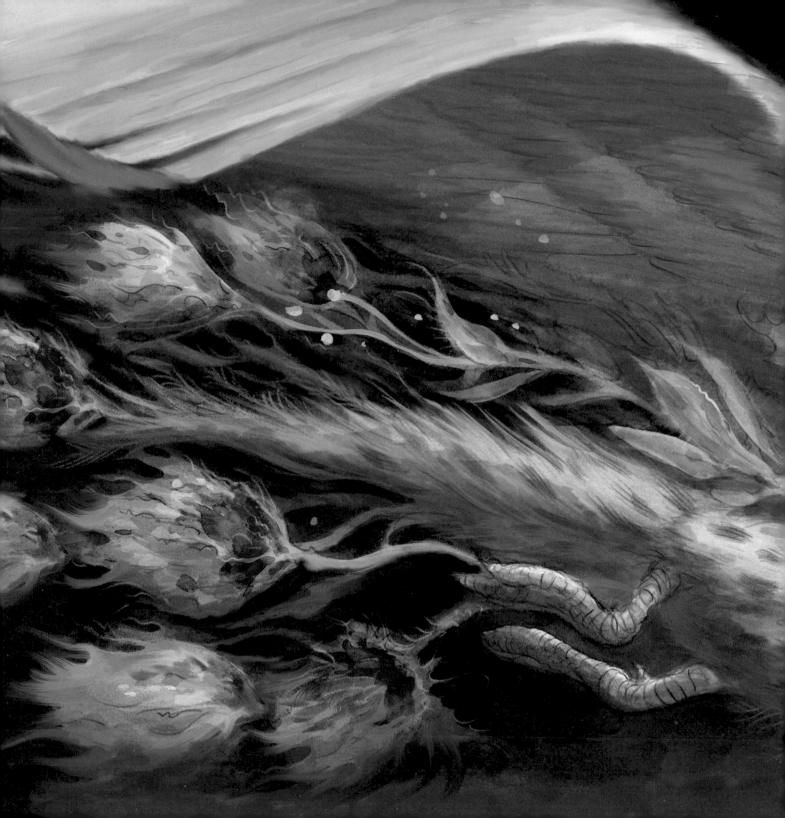

A confident you, strong and
brave too.

You being you is God's dream coming true.

'Cause when God made you, all of heaven was beaming.

Over YOU, God was smiling and already dreaming.